POPPY SEEDS, TOO
A Twisted Tale for Shabbat

POPPY SEEDS, TOO
A Twisted Tale for Shabbat

By Deborah Uchill Miller
Illustrated by Karen Ostrove

KAR-BEN COPIES, INC.   ROCKVILLE, MD

Library of Congress Cataloging in Publication Data

Miller, Deborah.
    Poppy seeds, too.

    Summary: Each one of several bakers contributes an original sug-
gestion to the recipe for challah, the special bread baked for the Sabbath.
    [1. Sabbath—Fiction. 2. Jews—Fiction. 3. Bread—Fiction. 4. Stories
in rhyme] I. Ostrove, Karen, ill.
II. Title.
PZ8.3.M61325Po   1982   [E]   82-84021
ISBN 0-930-49416-4
ISBN 0-930-49417-2 (pbk.)

ISBN 0-930-494-16-4—Cloth
ISBN 0-930-494-17-2—Paper
Library of Congress Catalog Number 82-84021

Published by KAR-BEN COPIES, INC.
Rockville, MD
Printed in the United States of America

for Clifford, a.k.a. Shaul
and Steve

As far back as any of us can remember,
Whether in April or May or December,

The Sabbath was different,
In winter or heat.
Not one bread, but two,
Made of whole wheat.

Every Shabbat
There were two loaves of bread.
Very nutritious,
But heavy as lead.

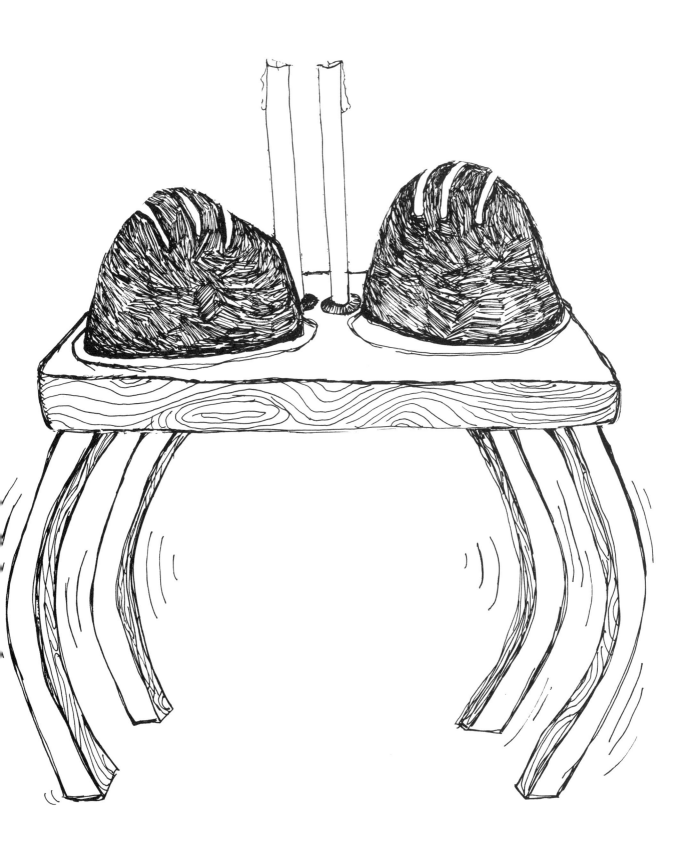

Then someone exclaimed,
"These loaves could be light!
To honor Shabbat,
Let's make them white."

"I have an idea!"
The shortest one said.
"We could add honey
To sweeten our bread."

The kitchen crowd gasped,
And you saw in their eyes
That the dozen fresh eggs
Were a thrilling surprise.

"We could add raisins,"
Went up the shout.

"But I don't like raisins."

"So just pick them out."

Sadie said, "That's enough!
We can stop working now.
Let's clean up my kitchen.
I'll show you all how."

"We'll clean up in a minute.
There's more we can do.

I have some alfalfa sprouts.
Add one or two."

"This bread is improved
Since the last time we made it.
But must it be round?
Why don't we braid it?"

Braid with three.   Braid with four.

Braid with six strands or more.

"I have an idea!"
The curly-head cried.
"Let's make it pretty
On the outside."

"We can glaze it with egg,
Add poppy seeds, too.
Put them on top,
We won't even need glue."

"Farewell," Sadie said.
"It's time that you go.
I'll bake all this challah
And scrape up the dough."

"Please let us back in!
We must cover the crust,
To protect our fresh challah
From sneezes and dust!"

"I'll tie-dye a cover."
"I'll fringe and batik it."
"I'll add some embroidery,
Bleach it, and streak it."

"A challah-board's needed.
We'll use it each week."
"I'll sand it."
"I'll carve it."
"We'll make it from teak."

"I know a great place
For wood we can share.
And for slicing the bread
Here's the leg of a chair."

"No!" cried a salesman.
"Not on your life.
What *this* challah needs
Is its very own knife."

He opened his coat
As he stood at the door.
"Come make your selection.
I've brought eighty-four."

We gathered in silence.
Our challah was glistening.
There were no new ideas.
Though all were still listening.

"I think we have finished,
This challah looks fine. . .

Now what can we do
To improve on the wine?"

THE KITCHEN CROWD'S CHALLAH

2 cups warm water
3 packages yeast
8-10 cups flour
⅓ cup sugar
1 tablespoon salt
2 sticks (½ lb.) margarine

4 eggs
⅓ cup honey
raisins (optional)
1 egg beaten with tablespoon of
water (for glaze)
poppy or sesame seeds (optional)

Mix the water and yeast in a very large bowl. Add the sugar and 3 cups of the flour. Stir well with a fork. Cover and let rise in a warm place for one hour.

Put 5 cups of flour and the salt in another bowl. Cut in the margarine as you would for pie crust, or blend in a food processor, until the mixture resembles coarse meal. Or you may melt the margarine, let it cool, and add it to the flour.

Add the honey and eggs to the yeast mixture, and stir well. Then add the flour mixture. Work into a ball, adding more flour as needed.

Turn out onto floured board and knead. Put in oiled bowl, cover, and let rise for 2 hours. Punch down. Divide the dough into parts. Add raisins if desired. Braid. Place on cookie sheet or in oiled loaf pans. Cover and let rise for one hour.

Brush tops with beaten egg. Sprinkle with poppy or sesame seeds. Bake in 325° oven for 20-40 minutes depending on size of loaf.

This process takes about 6 hours. However, there are periods of time when you may leave the dough alone to rise. The recipe makes enough for several loaves.

CHALLAH BLESSINGS

The word "challah" means dough. The Torah requires that a portion of one's bread dough be given to the Temple priests as a gift. Since the destruction of the Temple, this mitzvah is fulfilled by removing a small piece of dough before baking and burning it in the oven. We recite the following blessing:

בָּרוּךְ אַתָּה יְיָ אֱלֹהֵינוּ מֶלֶךְ הָעוֹלָם אֲשֶׁר קִדְּשָׁנוּ בְּמִצְוֹתָיו וְצִוָּנוּ לְהַפְרִישׁ חַלָּה

Baruch atah adonai eloheinu melech ha'olam asher kid'shanu b'mitzvotav v'tzivanu l'hafrish challah.

Blessed are You, O Lord our God, King of the universe, for the mitzvah of separating the challah.

Before we enjoy the challah, we recite another blessing:

בָּרוּךְ אַתָּה יְיָ אֱלֹהֵינוּ מֶלֶךְ הָעוֹלָם הַמּוֹצִיא לֶחֶם מִן הָאָרֶץ

Baruch atah adonai eloheinu melech ha'olam hamotzi lechem min ha'aretz.

Blessed are You, O Lord our God, King of the universe, who brings forth bread from the earth.

ABOUT THE AUTHOR

Deborah Uchill Miller has lived, studied, taught, rebbitzined, and baked challah for her husband, Rabbi Clifford Miller, and daughters, Arielle and Adinah, in Denver, New York, Texas, Thailand, Nebraska, Maryland, Philadelphia, Jerusalem, New Jersey, and now Minneapolis, where she directs the Shabbat Morning Program at Adath Jeshurun Synagogue.

ABOUT THE ILLUSTRATOR

Karen Davis Ostrove, a former second grade teacher, began her free-lance art career illustrating lunch bags for her three children. A native New Yorker, she lives with her biochemist husband, Steve, and children in Elizabeth, New Jersey.

Deborah and Karen also created the enormously popular *Only Nine Chairs—A Tall Tale for Passover.*